THE RULER OF THE SPRINGS

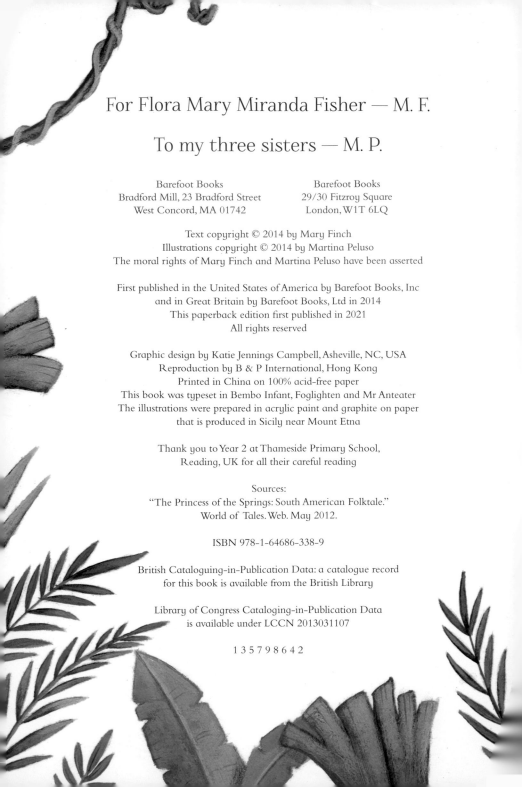

For Flora Mary Miranda Fisher — M. F.

To my three sisters — M. P.

Barefoot Books
Bradford Mill, 23 Bradford Street
West Concord, MA 01742

Barefoot Books
29/30 Fitzroy Square
London, W1T 6LQ

First published in the United States of America by Barefoot Books, Inc
and in Great Britain by Barefoot Books, Ltd in 2014
This paperback edition first published in 2021

Graphic design by Katie Jennings Campbell, Asheville, NC, USA
Reproduction by B & P International, Hong Kong
Printed in China on 100% acid-free paper
This book was typeset in Bembo Infant, Foglighten and Mr Anteater
The illustrations were prepared in acrylic paint and graphite on paper
that is produced in Sicily near Mount Etna

Thank you to Year 2 at Thameside Primary School,
Reading, UK for all their careful reading

Sources:
"The Princess of the Springs: South American Folktale."
World of Tales. Web. May 2012.

ISBN 978-1-64686-338-9

British Cataloguing-in-Publication Data: a catalogue record
for this book is available from the British Library

Library of Congress Cataloging-in-Publication Data
is available under LCCN 2013031107

1 3 5 7 9 8 6 4 2

THE Ruler OF THE Springs

A Tale from Brazil

Retold by **Mary Finch**

Illustrated by **Martina Peluso**

Barefoot Books
step inside a story

CONTENTS

CHAPTER 1
Princess Ibura

Once upon a time, when the world was young, the Moon Giant fell in love with the giantess who lived in the Great River. He built her a palace made of shells and silver and sparkling gems.

After a while, a baby girl was born to
the Moon Giant and the Giantess of the
Great River. Her eyes shone like the moon
and she was as strong as the Great River.
They called her Ibura, the Ruler of the
Springs. She was the princess of all the
springs, rivers and lakes in the land.

Ibura grew up to be beautiful, clever and wise. Her father lived in the night sky and she lived with her mother in the silver and shell palace. She wanted to stay there forever.

But the Sun Giant had seen the Ruler of the Springs in the waters of the rivers and streams as he crossed the sky every day. She was so beautiful that he fell in love with her. "Ah," he said. "That is the wife for me." He knocked on the door of the silver and shell palace and asked her to marry him.

"Oh, no," said Ibura. "I don't want to leave my mother."

But the Sun Giant had made up his mind. And being so strong and brave, he was used to getting his own way. Every day he asked Ibura to be his wife and live with him in his gold palace in the sky. Each time she said no, but each time he looked so sad that she began to care for him.

"Yes, I will marry you and live in your
gold palace in the sky," she said at last, "but
only if for three months of every year I can
go home to my mother, the Giantess of the
Great River, and the shell palace."

CHAPTER 2

The Gold Palace

So the Sun Giant and Ibura, the Ruler of the Springs, were married. They went to live in the gold palace in the sky. They were happy together.

The Sun Giant was kind and strong, but Ibura missed her mother. For three months each year she went home, and for those three months the Great River and the other rivers and lakes shone and sparkled with joy.

A baby son was born to Ibura and the Sun Giant. Ibura wanted to take him to the silver and shell palace and show him to the Giantess of the Great River. But the Sun Giant said she must leave their son with him.

"The prince must stay at home in the gold palace," he said. "He is too little to make the journey all the way down to the Great River with you."

Ibura was very sad. She loved her son
and would miss him while she was gone.
But she knew the Sun Giant would take
care of him and she agreed that the prince
should stay at the gold palace.

18

CHAPTER 3
In Prison

Ibura set off for the silver and shell palace, but when she arrived her mother was not there. The princess ran into every room. She called, "Mother, where are you?" But there was no answer.

The princess asked the fish in the Great

River if they had seen her mother.

"No," they answered. "We haven't seen her."

20

The princess asked the sands on the
seashore if they had seen her mother.

"No," they answered. "We haven't seen her."

She asked the yellow shells on the
seashore if they had seen her mother.

"Ask the Giant of the Wind," they
said. "He goes everywhere and knows
everything."

The princess did not know what else to do. She went to the house of the Giant of the Wind. "Do you know where my mother is?" she asked him.

The Giant of the Wind promised he would look for the Giantess of the Great River. He blew over the hills and the forests and at last he came to the castle of the Giant of the Land.

The Giant of the Wind blew into every crack of the castle. In the deep dungeon he found Ibura's mother. The Giant of the Land had put the giantess in prison in the darkest part of his castle. He wanted to take the shell palace and the river for himself.

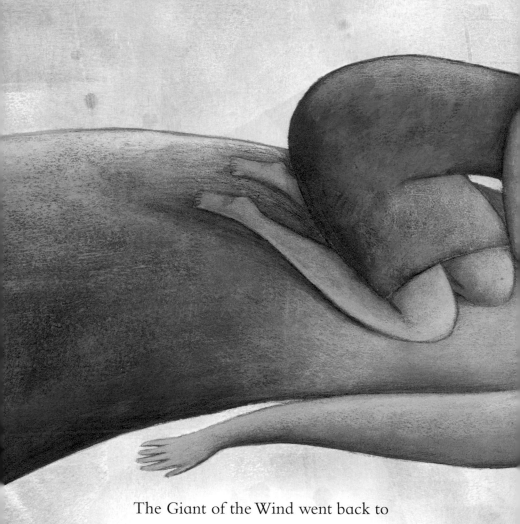

The Giant of the Wind went back to
his house. He told the Ruler of the Springs
that he had found her mother. He put the
princess on his back and together they flew
to the Giant of the Land's castle.

29

"Give me back my mother," said the
Ruler of the Springs.

"No," said the Giant of the Land. "She is
mine now and I will keep her."

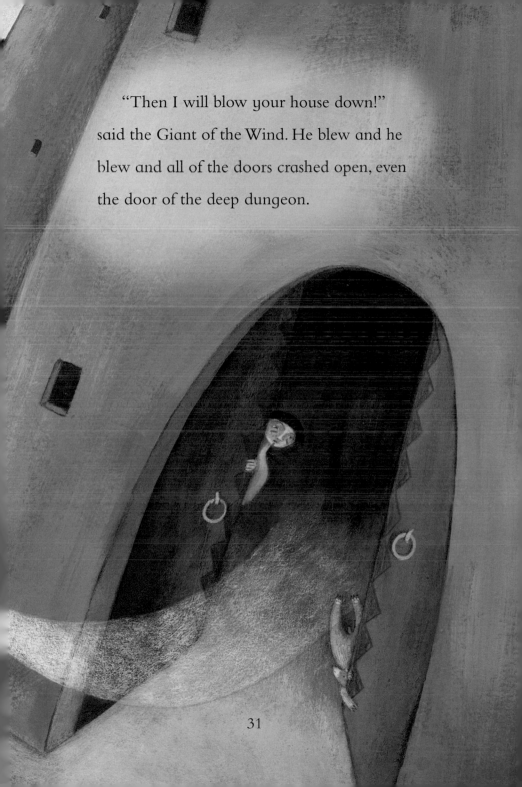

"Then I will blow your house down!" said the Giant of the Wind. He blew and he blew and all of the doors crashed open, even the door of the deep dungeon.

31

The Giantess of the Great River was
very happy to see her daughter. She had not
liked the dark dungeon and longed to be
in the open air again. Ibura led her mother
outside and hugged her.

The princess and the Giantess of the
Great River thanked the Giant of the Wind
for his help. They went back to the shell
palace. They had been away for more than
three months.

"The Sun Giant will not know where I
am. He will miss me," said Ibura. "And my
son will miss me too. I must go home."

CHAPTER 4
The Lost Prince

The Sun Giant was very upset when the
Ruler of the Springs did not come home
after three months. Instead of looking for
Ibura, he married another wife. The new
wife was jealous of the little prince. She sent
him away, out into the sky.

But the cook felt sorry for the little
prince. He saw how lost and lonely he
was out in the clouds. The cook took the
prince back to the palace and hid him in
the kitchen. The prince played with the
dogs and ate the scraps that the kind cook
gave him. The little prince was so dirty that
nobody knew who he was.

When the Ruler of the Springs arrived
back at the palace of the Sun Giant, she
called out for her son. The little prince was
not there. One of the palace servants began
to cry and told the princess how the new
wife had sent him away.

"Where is he?" the princess asked.

"I don't know," said the poor servant.

"Then we must find him at once," said the princess. And she ran through the gardens and the palace calling for her little boy, but it did no good.

The princess was so sad that she went back to the Great River to be with her mother. There she wept and wept and wept for forty days.

And as she wept, her tears made the
Great River flood into the sea, and the sea
rose so high that it covered the gold palace
of the Sun Giant.

For forty days the palace of the Sun
Giant, and everyone inside, was covered by
the sea. The Sun Giant could not shine on
the earth and the land was dark.

CHAPTER 5
The Giant of the Rain

The prince was very sad too. He missed
his mother, the Ruler of the Springs, and
he didn't want to stay in the palace kitchen
with just the dogs and the cook for friends
and scraps for food.

He left the palace and set off into the
clouds where he began to cry. His tears
washed his face clean and fell all the way
down to the earth.

Ibura felt the tears dropping around her. She looked up and saw her son crying. She rushed up into the sky as fast as she could to bring him home.

She picked the prince up and hugged
him. He told her how the kind cook had
hidden him, but how he missed her and was
always hungry.

Then the Ruler of the Springs dried her
tears, took the little prince by the hand and
went home to the silver and shell palace
and the Giantess of the Great River. There
she stayed and she didn't go back to the
Sun Giant.

The little prince grew up to be the Giant of the Rain. When rain falls on the earth in the rainy season it is him, dropping tears like he did when his mother was far away and he was sad and all alone. And the thirsty land welcomes the rain, the crops grow tall and strong, and the Ruler of the Springs makes the rivers and lakes sparkle with joy.